P9-BZM-570

characters created by
lauren child

This
is ACTUALLY
my
Party

Grosset & Dunlap

Charlie ♥ and Lola™

Text based on scripts Written by Dave Ingham

Illustrations from the TV animation produced by Tiger Aspect

GROSSET & DUNLAP
Published by the Penguin Group
Penguin Group (USA) Inc., 375 Hudson Street, New York, New York 10014, USA
Penguin Group (Canada), 90 Eglinton Avenue East, Suite 700, Toronto, Ontario M4P 2Y3, Canada
(a division of Pearson Penguin Canada Inc.)
Penguin Books Ltd., 80 Strand, London WC2R 0RL, England
Penguin Group Ireland, 25 St. Stephen's Green, Dublin 2, Ireland
(a division of Penguin Books Ltd.)
Penguin Group (Australia), 250 Camberwell Road, Camberwell, Victoria 3124, Australia
(a division of Pearson Australia Group Pty. Ltd.)
Penguin Books India Pvt. Ltd., 11 Community Centre, Panchsheel Park, New Delhi—110 017, India
Penguin Group (NZ), 67 Apollo Drive, Rosedale, North Shore 0745, Auckland, New Zealand
(a division of Pearson New Zealand Ltd.)
Penguin Books (South Africa) (Pty.) Ltd., 24 Sturdee Avenue,
Rosebank, Johannesburg 2196, South Africa

Penguin Books Ltd., Registered Offices:
80 Strand, London WC2R 0RL, England

First published as *This is Actually My Party* in Great Britain 2007 by Puffin Books.

Library of Congress Control Number: 2007012935

ISBN 978-0-448-44694-3   10 9 8 7 6 5 4 3 2 1

I have this little sister, Lola.
        She is small and very funny.
        Today is my birthday, and I'm having a party.
All my friends are invited.
        All my friends and Lola!

"Look at all your **birthday cards**, Charlie . . ."

"Lola!" I say.

"You opened MY cards!"

And Lola says,
"I know, but Mum said I should help
make sure you have an
EXTREMELY lovely happy birthday.

That's why I helped you
open your cards."

"There's going
to be lots
of presents..."
says Lola.

"Oh, I can't wait!
I can't wait!"

"And
lots of
party
games.

Like
musical
statues!"

"And of course the **cake**!
I love
birthday parties!"
says Lola.   "Oh, I can't wait!
I can't wait!"

Then I say,
"Well, my **party's** not going
to be quite like that, Lola . . .

. . . because LOOK!
Mum has made me
a special **cake**
because MY party is
a **monster** party."

Lola says,
"It's a shame there's
no **pink** icing."

I say,
"That's because
it's a **monster cake**
and **monsters**
hate pink."

When everything is ready,
Dad says he'll take me to the store,
to get my own **scary** mask.

I say to Lola,
"Do you want
to come, too?"

Lola says,
"No, thank you,
Charlie

I'm going to help
Mum make more
party things."

"Pink is definitely for parties!

Yes,

pink,
    pink,
pink.

Charlie's
going to be
SO pleased."

When I get back from the store,
we put on our **party** costumes
and wait for my friends to arrive.

Then we hear a knock
at the door.

"I'll get it," says Lola.

I say,
"Wow, thanks for
coming, everyone!
We've got **monster** drinks.
Come on in!"

But then Lola says,
"Look at Marv's present,
Charlie!

It's
a
TELE-SPOKE!"

"Lola!" I say.
"Please let ME unwrap
MY **presents** myself."

And Lola says,
"Okay, Charlie,
I'm just helping."

Then I say,
"My dad's set up all the
games for us
in the garden.

There's **monster** tag
and
monster chase . . ."

"Musical statues, everyone!"
says Lola.

"Ready,

steady,

GO!"

"No musical statues, Lola.
We're going to play MY **monster** games outside."

Then Marv says,
    "Are we going to have any **cake**?"
And I say,
    "Oh yes, wait till you see it!"

"Happy birthday, Charlie!

Lola says,
"What's wrong, Charlie?"

So I say,
"ONE.
You open all my cards.

TWO.
You open my present from Marv.

THREE.
You make everyone
play YOUR
party games.

And . . . and . . . FOUR . . .
You blow out my candles!

This is

my party,
not your party!"

Lola says,
   "I just like parties."

"I know you like parties, Lola. But this is actually my party."

Lola says,
   "I'm sorry."

And I say,
   "Well, at least you didn't give anyone pink fairy cakes."

Then we go to play monster freeze tag outside.

"Charlie, Charlie! Save me before Frankenstein gets me!"

While we are playing **monster** tag,
Lola has an idea . . .

"Monsters,
monsters,
monsters."

When we go back inside . . .

. . . Lola has made **monster party**
goodie bags for all my friends!
Lola says, "Thank you for
coming to Charlie's **party**."

Then Marv sees Lola's **fairy cakes**.
"Oh, can I have one of those?"

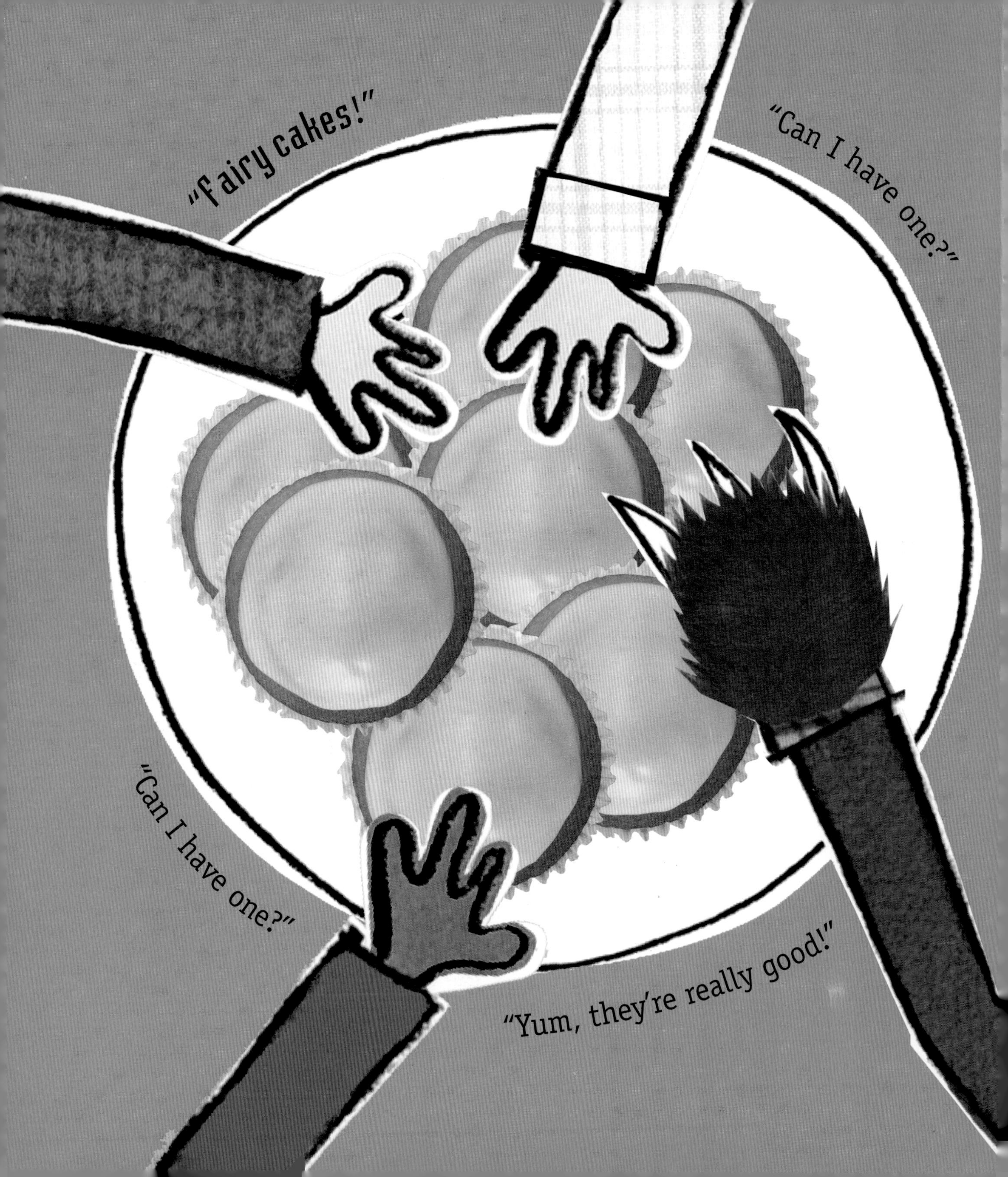
"Fairy cakes!"
"Can I have one?"
"Can I have one?"
"Yum, they're really good!"

And Marv says,
"Thank you, Lola.
Pink icing is really tasty."

Later, Lola says,
"That was a REALLY good party, wasn't it?"
            And I say, "That was a REALLY good party."
Lola says, "They REALLY liked my pink fairy cakes!"
            And I say,
"Even monsters think pink icing is the tastiest!"